Anthony and the Aardvark

Anthony and the Aardvark

Lesley Sloss · Gus Clarke

Andersen Press · London

10 9 8 7 6 5 4 3 2 1

British Library Cataloguing in Publication Data available.

ISBN 0 86264 877 7

This book has been printed on acid-free paper

This is Mr and Mrs Jones, Anthony's grandpa and grandma.
Mr and Mrs Jones look after Anthony when Anthony's parents
are busy.

This is Anthony.

This is a baby aardvark. Very different, aren't they? Mr and Mrs Jones have very bad eyesight.

This is what Anthony and the baby aardvark look like to them. Very similar, aren't they?

It is perhaps not so surprising to hear, then,
that one Saturday Mr and Mrs Jones got Anthony
and the baby aardvark mixed up. It all started
when Mr and Mrs Jones decided to take Anthony
to the zoo.

Anthony had never been to the zoo before. He saw lots of new animals — lions, tigers, bears, elephants and kangaroos and lots more. Mr and Mrs Jones saw lots of things, too, but not as many as Anthony saw.

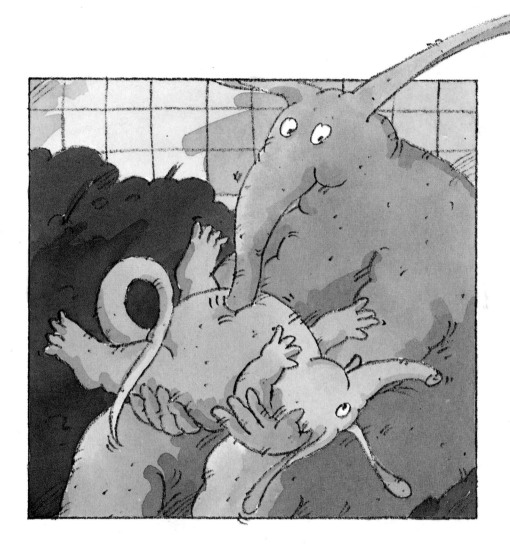

Anthony's favourite animals in the whole zoo were the
aardvark mummy and its new baby. The mummy aardvark
was using her long furry snout to tickle the baby's tummy until
it grunted and squeaked with delight.

Anthony watched the aardvarks for a long time wishing he was having his tummy tickled. It looked such fun.

The baby aardvark stared back at Anthony. He had seen many
children staring at him before through the cage bars. Most of them
carried food. The baby aardvark wished he could have some
of the ice-cream they clutched in their hands.

There was a hole in the fence of the aardvarks' cage. Anthony could see it. The baby aardvark could see it. Mr and Mrs Jones couldn't see it. And they didn't notice Anthony crawling through the hole into the aardvarks' cage and the baby aardvark crawling out.

Mr and Mrs Jones took the aardvark home instead of Anthony, by mistake.

Soon Anthony was being tickled, just as he had wanted. The mummy aardvark didn't seem to notice that her baby was now Anthony. Aardvarks aren't short sighted, they just aren't very clever.

When Mr and Mrs Jones got home they sat the baby aardvark in Anthony's high chair and gave it some tomato soup. The baby aardvark didn't like the soup. He stuck his tongue out at it. Aardvarks have very long tongues and no table manners.

Back at the zoo the mummy aardvark had put
some ants down for Anthony. Anthony couldn't
catch the ants and he was very sure he didn't
want to eat them.

After lunch Mrs Jones tucked the baby aardvark
snugly into bed for an afternoon nap. The baby
aardvark couldn't sleep. He didn't like the
look that Anthony's teddy bear kept giving him.

When the mummy aardvark went into her burrow for
an afternoon nap, Anthony stayed outside. He was
scared that the burrow might contain more ants.

After his rest, the baby aardvark was taken into the bathroom and put into a warm tub of soapy water. He'd never had a bath before. He liked the bubbles and the yellow plastic duck but he hated the soap. It tasted terrible.

After his rest, Anthony always looked forward to his warm, soapy bath. Instead, he was licked clean by the mummy aardvark's long pink tongue. He hated it. Perhaps being an aardvark wasn't so much fun after all.

The first moment that Mrs Jones realised that there was something
wrong was when she played the piggy game. She and Anthony
always played after Anthony's bath. She started,
"This little piggy went to market,
 This little piggy stayed at home,
 This little piggy had roast beef,
 This little piggy had none,
 And this . . ."
But there were no more piggies! The baby aardvark only had four
toes. Mrs Jones called Mr Jones into the living room and together
they had a good look to see what was wrong with Anthony.

"Oh dear," said Mrs Jones, "he seems to have very big ears."
"And a very big nose," said Mr Jones.
"And he's sticking his tongue out," said Mrs Jones in surprise.
Anthony was not normally as rude as this in front of his grandparents.

"It's not Anthony!" they gasped together.
"It's a rabbit," said Mrs Jones.
"No, it's a badger," cried Mr Jones.
"Whatever it is, it's certainly not Anthony," said Mrs Jones.
"We must have muddled them up at the zoo."

Mr and Mrs Jones went back to the zoo as quickly as they could. They put a hat and coat on the baby aardvark so that people wouldn't stare at them too much.

Once Anthony saw Mr and Mrs Jones arriving at the aardvarks'
cage he crawled back through the hole as fast as he could.
He had never felt so pleased to see them as he felt now.

The baby aardvark crawled out of the clothes it was wearing and ran back to snuggle up to its mummy.

It was good to be back home again.

More Andersen Press paperback picture books!